My Secret Unicorn

Unicorn

A Special Friend

The pony looked at her
with sad, dark eyes, and a memory
stirred in Lauren's mind. The very first
time she had seen Twilight, he had looked
at her in exactly the same way. It was so
weird. . . . A thought struck Lauren and
she almost gasped out loud. No, she
couldn't be right. . . .

My Secret Unicorn

A Special Friend

Linda Chapman

Illustrated by Biz Hull

Cover Illustration by Andrew Farley

AN
APPLE
PAPERBACK

SCHOLASTIC INC.

New York Toronto London Auckland Sydney
Mexico City New Delhi Hong Kong Buenos Aires

ISBN 0-439-70124-4

12 11 10 9 8 7 6 5 4 3 2 1   4   5   6   7 8/0

Printed in the U.S.A.   40

First Scholastic printing, November 2004

To Michelle Mistra — for making
My Secret Unicorn *so magical*

CHAPTER

One

"Lauren! Are you ready? The Parkers are here!" Mrs. Foster said, looking out the kitchen window.

Lauren fed the remains of her toast to Buddy, her brother Max's young Bernese mountain dog. He gobbled up the crusts with a gulp and then bounded around in front of her.

"Out of the way, Buddy!" Lauren said,

laughing. She grabbed her riding hat from the table. "See you later, Mom."

"Have fun!" Mrs. Foster called.

"I will." Lauren hurried out of the

house to the car. Her friend Jessica sat in the back with her stepsister, Samantha. They were going to choose a pony and Lauren was helping them!

"Hello, Lauren," Mr. Parker said, smiling at her as she got into the back of the car.

"Hi," Lauren said. She exchanged grins with Jessica and Samantha. They were both looking very excited.

Mr. Parker started the engine. "OK, everyone. High Meadows Farm, here we come."

The stables were a fifteen-minute drive from Lauren's house on the outskirts of

town. A signpost at the top of the farm's
driveway read:

> ## High Meadows
> ## — riding school and pony sales
> ## Proprietor: T. Bradshaw

At the end of the driveway were two red
barns, an office, and a large training ring.

As Mr. Parker stopped the car, a
woman with curly auburn hair came out
of the office. "Hi there," she said, smiling
as they piled out of the car. "You must be
the Parkers?"

Mr. Parker nodded. "Yes, this is Samantha
and Jessica and Jessica's friend Lauren."

"I'm Tina Bradshaw," the woman said.

She glanced at Jessica and Samantha. "So, you're looking for a pony?"

They both nodded.

Tina smiled. "Then come with me — I have plenty for you to see."

She led the way across the yard and into the first barn. On either side of the wide central aisle, ponies peered over half doors, their ears pricked.

"I'll show you the ponies I think might be most suitable and then you can choose three or four you'd like to try out in the ring," Tina said. She headed over to a stall where a chestnut with a white blaze was looking out. "This is Puzzle. He's ten years old and a very good jumper. Next to him is . . ."

Lauren's brain was soon spinning with pony names. After looking at twelve ponies in the barn, Samantha and Jessica had chosen four to ride — Bullfinch, Puzzle, Lacey, and Sandy. Tina saddled them and led them to the training ring.

"Why don't you try Puzzle first?" she said to Jessica, handing her the reins of the chestnut. "And Samantha, you try Bullfinch."

Lauren watched as Samantha and Jessica took turns riding the ponies around the ring. All of them looked great and she didn't know which one she'd choose if it were up to her.

Seeing some ponies looking over the

gate of a field a little way off, Lauren wandered over to see them. There was a palomino — tan-colored with a pale gold mane and tail — a bay, and a black. Lauren stroked them and then she noticed another pony — a shaggy little dapple-gray — standing all by herself farther up the field.

Lauren stared. The dapple-gray was exactly like her pony, Twilight! Although Twilight looked like an ordinary pony, he had an exciting secret. At certain times of the day, Lauren could say the words of the Turning Spell, which transformed Twilight into a unicorn!

Lauren hurried around the fence. As she got closer, she saw that the dapple-gray pony was a bit smaller and scruffier than Twilight, but otherwise just like him. She even had the same pattern of dapples on her coat.

Lauren picked a handful of long grass. "Here," she called, holding the grass out. "Here, girl."

The gray mare lifted her head slightly.

"Come on," Lauren encouraged.

The mare walked over. Stopping by the fence, she reached out and took the grass, her soft gray lips nuzzling Lauren's palm.

On her halter was a brass nameplate. "Moonshine," Lauren read aloud. "Is that your name?"

The pony looked at her with sad, dark

eyes, and a
memory stirred
in Lauren's mind.
The very first
time she had seen
Twilight, he had
looked at her in

exactly the same way. It was so weird. He
and this pony were so alike that they
might almost be brother and sister. A
thought struck Lauren and she almost
gasped out loud. No, she couldn't be
right. . . .

"Moonshine, are . . . are you a unicorn
in disguise, just like Twilight?" she
whispered.

CHAPTER

Two

Moonshine stared at Lauren. "I know about unicorns," Lauren said quickly. "I have one myself."

"Lauren!" Hearing Jessica, Lauren turned.

"Come tell me which pony you like best," Jessica called to her.

Lauren didn't want to leave Moonshine. "Just a minute," she replied. She looked at the little gray pony again. "I won't tell anyone," she whispered. "Please — are you a unicorn?"

Moonshine didn't move.

"Lauren!" Jessica called impatiently.

Lauren gave up on getting Moonshine to respond. "Coming!" She hurried back to the ring, her thoughts racing.

Jessica was riding Sandy around the ring for a second time. Seeing Lauren coming over, she called out, "Watch how Sandy goes and then you can tell me which pony you like best."

Lauren nodded and went to stand by Tina at the gate.

Tina smiled at her. "I saw you talking to Moonshine just now."

"She's lovely," Lauren said.

Tiny nodded. "I think so, too, but no one ever wants to buy her. I guess she doesn't look flashy enough. It's a shame — she's got a heart of gold. You're not looking for a pony, are you?"

Lauren shook her head regretfully. She would have loved to buy Moonshine but she knew her parents would never agree.

"Pity," Tina sighed. "Moonshine could use some love. The girls who help out here prefer riding the livelier ponies, and she doesn't get much attention. Oh, well." She turned away to speak to Mr. Parker.

Jessica rode over. "So, which do you like best?" she asked eagerly.

"I like them all," Lauren said truthfully. She watched the palomino Jessica was riding. "Sandy's very pretty."

"She's my favorite," Jessica confided. "But I think Sam likes Bullfinch." She looked curiously at Tina. "What were you and Tina talking about?"

"About that pony over there," Lauren

said, pointing to Moonshine, who was still standing by the fence in the field.

Jessica stared. "Isn't she sweet? She looks just like Twilight!"

Lauren nodded.

"I'll ask if we can try her out," Jessica said.

Lauren felt a leap of excitement. If Moonshine was a unicorn and Jessica bought her, it would be amazing! But to Lauren's disappointment, when Jessica asked, Tina shook her head.

"Moonshine will be too small for Samantha," she told Jessica. "She's only twelve-point-two hands high. You need a pony who's at least thirteen-point-two."

"Oh," Jessica said, looking at Lauren.

"OK, Samantha," Mr. Parker called. "Come over here. It's decision time."

Samantha rode over on Bullfinch.

"So which pony will it be?" Mr. Parker asked her and Jessica.

"Sandy," Jessica said immediately.

"Bullfinch," said Samantha at the same moment.

"Not Bullfinch," Jessica put in quickly. "He's too heavy and slow."

"He's obedient and reliable," Samantha said, patting the buckskin's neck. "Not like Sandy. She refused when I tried to jump her."

"She didn't with me," Jessica said.

"Fluke," Samantha said.

"It *wasn't*!" Jessica declared hotly.

"Sandy's only young," Tina said. "She's still learning about jumping, so she might stop a little more than an experienced pony. But once she gets used to jumps she should be just fine."

"Well, I want Bullfinch," Samantha announced.

"And I want Sandy!" Jessica frowned.

Mr. Parker looked at Tina. "I'm sorry about this — there seems to be some disagreement."

"That's OK," Tina said understandingly. "Buying a pony is a big commitment. You have to be sure you're getting the right one. How about you talk it over tonight and come back tomorrow? You can try them both out again then."

Mr. Parker looked relieved. "Are you sure that would be OK?"

Tina nodded. "No problem."

As soon as Lauren got home, she raced to Twilight's field and told him all about Moonshine.

"So, what do you think?" she

demanded eagerly. "Do you think she
might be a unicorn?"

Twilight stamped a hoof. Lauren
wished she could turn him into a
unicorn so that they could really speak,
but she knew her dad was working
nearby so she couldn't risk it. "We'll

talk about it tonight, when it starts to get dark," she promised.

It was nearly twilight, and Lauren went back to the house. She grabbed a can of lemonade from the fridge and went up to her bedroom. This was her favorite place in the whole house. It had a sloping ceiling and a large window with a window seat that looked down on Twilight's paddock. Lauren looked out. Twilight was grazing in the shade of the trees. He looked happy. She blew him a kiss before picking up an old blue book that was lying on the window seat. It was called *The Life of a Unicorn* and it had been given to her by Mrs. Fontana, an older

woman who owned a bookshop. Mrs.
Fontana was the only other person in the
world who knew the truth about Twilight.

Sitting down, Lauren curled her legs
underneath her and carefully opened up
the book. After Twilight, it was one of
her most treasured possessions. In the back
of it were the words of the Turning Spell.

Lauren leafed carefully
through the book, her
eyes scanning the
yellowing, faded
pages. At last, she
found what she
was looking for:
a picture of a

little gray pony. It was a unicorn in its
pony form.

She turned back a page and read the
words.

> *Descendants of the two young unicorns that*
> *Noah took onto the Ark still roam the earth*
> *today. They look like small ponies. Each of*
> *them hopes to find someone who will learn*
> *how to free them from their mortal form.*

Lauren turned again to the picture of the
small gray pony. Both Twilight and
Moonshine looked just like it. Lauren
stared out the window, frowning slightly.
Was Moonshine a unicorn? She and
Twilight had to find out!

★   ★   ★

As soon as she could that evening, Lauren rushed out to find Twilight. Quickly, she said the words of the Turning Spell that changed him into a unicorn:

Twilight Star, Twilight Star,
Twinkling high above so far.
Shining light, shining bright,
Will you grant my wish tonight?
Let my little horse forlorn
Be at last a unicorn!

With a bright purple flash, Twilight stood before her in his unicorn form.

"Well, what do you think?" Lauren asked again.

"I need to see her before I can tell," Twilight replied.

"OK, let's fly over there now," Lauren said. She looked up at the dusky sky. "It's dark enough, and Mom and Dad won't miss me. Mom's busy working and Dad's watching a movie on TV."

She scrambled onto Twilight's back and, with a snort, he jumped up into the sky. He cantered toward the sliver of moon that had started to shine above the trees.

"Which way is it?" Twilight asked.

"Just out of town, to the north," Lauren said, her hair blowing back from her face. "It should be really quick to fly there. The roads took us a very twisty way around."

She was right. Flying direct, they reached High Meadows Farm in five minutes.

Lauren scanned the ground. The only things moving seemed to be ponies. Tina and her helpers had probably gone home for the night.

"I think we can go down," she said to Twilight. "It's that field over there by the training ring. Look, there she is — the little gray standing all by herself."

As Twilight swooped down, the palomino, bay, and black ponies scattered to the far side of the field with snorts of alarm. But Moonshine didn't move. She stared at Twilight as if transfixed. Her dark eyes grew wider and then she lifted

her head and arched her neck. Shaking
back her mane, Moonshine stepped
toward Twilight, her delicate ears
pricked, her hooves moving daintily on
the grass. She looked so graceful with the
moonlight shining on her pale coat that
Lauren didn't need Twilight to tell her
what he thought. Moonshine *was* a
unicorn. She knew it beyond a doubt.

Twilight whinnied softly. Moonshine
whickered back and as she reached him,
they extended their heads and touched
noses.

"Unicorn," Lauren heard Twilight
murmur.

Moonshine snorted and looked at
Lauren.

"What's she saying?" Lauren asked.

"She's saying you told her that you had a unicorn," Twilight translated. Moonshine whimpered sadly.

"She has never found anyone to be her Unicorn Friend," Twilight said. "It's all she's ever dreamed of."

Lauren felt desperately sorry for the little pony. She knew that for a unicorn to be freed from its pony form, it needed to find a special person — a special person who believed in magic. Then they could share magical adventures together. "Please tell her she will find someone to be her Unicorn Friend," Lauren urged. She reached forward and patted Moonshine.

"You'll find someone who believes in magic. I know it."

Lauren spoke determinedly, but inside she was far from sure. *I hope I'm right,* she thought.

Moonshine bowed her head and snorted quietly.

"She says she doesn't think it will happen," Twilight said softly.

Looking at the dejected little pony, Lauren wanted to help her more than anything else in the world. Sliding off Twilight's back, she went over and stroked Moonshine's neck to comfort her. Moonshine looked up at her, her dark eyes like deep forest pools.

Suddenly, there was a change in her. Moonshine's ears pricked and she stiffened. She glanced around to the gate and then, turning back to Twilight, she snorted anxiously.

Lauren saw a look of alarm cross Twilight's face.

"Quick, Lauren," he said. "There's someone coming!"

CHAPTER
Three

"Over there!" Lauren said, pointing to a nearby wooded area.

Lauren swiftly mounted and Twilight galloped among the trees. They were just in time. As they reached the shadows, they saw a boy walk up to the gate and climb over it. Lauren and Twilight waited in the trees, watching without being seen.

The boy headed toward Moonshine.

He was skinny with untidy dark hair. He wasn't very tall but, judging by his face, Lauren guessed that he was probably about her age.

"Here, Moonshine," she heard him say. He held out a handful of carrots. "Here, beauty."

Moonshine walked over to the boy. He fed her the carrots and stroked her tangled mane. "Did you think I wasn't coming?"

Moonshine snorted.

Lauren bent low on Twilight's neck. "Who is he?" she whispered. "Did Moonshine say?"

"She doesn't know," Twilight replied. "She told me he started coming a few days ago — he's here for the summer with his family. He always brings her something to eat and just spends time talking to her and stroking her. Moonshine likes him."

Lauren watched the boy talking softly to Moonshine and suddenly made a decision. "Wait here," she said to Twilight as she dismounted and walked out of the trees.

The boy almost jumped out of his skin. He stared at her in surprise, then turned and began to run across the field.

"Please, wait!" Lauren called, chasing after him.

But the boy didn't stop. He raced to the gate.

"Wait!" Lauren implored him, panting for breath as she ran after him. "I only want to talk to you!"

Glancing over his shoulder, the boy tripped over a tree root and fell. It gave Lauren the time she needed to catch up with him. She grabbed his arm.

"I wasn't doing anything!" He gasped, his face pale, his brown shock of hair sticking up. "I was just talking to the pony. I wasn't hurting her, I promise."

"I know you weren't," Lauren said. "It's OK."

The boy stared at her carefully for the first time. "You're . . . you're not angry with me for feeding her?"

"No," Lauren said in surprise. "Of course not." She let him go and they both stood up.

"Is it your pony?" he asked.

Lauren shook her head. "No. She belongs to Tina, the woman who owns these stables." She frowned. "Who are you? What are you doing here?"

"My name's Michael," the boy said warily. "If Moonshine's not your pony, what are *you* doing in the field?"

Lauren didn't know what to reply. "I . . . er . . . I was here today," she said, "with some friends who are buying a pony. I saw Moonshine and liked her. I thought I'd come back and visit." At least it was half the truth.

Michael relaxed and, for the first time, he smiled at her. "That's why I'm here, too," he confessed. "I was exploring a few days ago and I saw Moonshine in the field. I thought she looked kind of lonely so I started to visit her. I've been coming every day. So, where do you live?" Michael asked out of curiosity.

"Not too far away," Lauren said vaguely, thinking: *if you fly here.* "How about you?" she asked, changing the subject.

"Me?" Michael hesitated for a moment. "In Washington," he replied. "Only I'm staying in a house nearby for

the summer with my mom and dad.
We've done a house swap with a
colleague of Jodie's . . . I mean my
mom's." He glanced at her, wondering
whether to say more. "Jodie's my adoptive
mom," Michael explained after a pause. "I
haven't been with them long. My real
mom died two years ago and I was put
into foster care."

Lauren didn't know what to say. "I'm
really s-sorry," she stammered.

Michael gazed down. "It's OK."

He looked up and smiled as
Moonshine walked over to him, her
hooves echoing softly on the grass.

Moonshine snorted softly and rubbed
her head against Michael's chest. He

scratched her ears. There was silence for a moment.

"It must be strange moving to the country just for the summer," Lauren said sympathetically.

"Yes, it is," Michael admitted. "It's hard to fit in and make new friends when everyone's already settled." He tried to look cheerful. "But at least I get to see horses — you don't see many of them in the city." He stroked Moonshine's face. "I really wish I could have a pony of my own. I stayed on a farm for a while when I was being fostered. The people there taught me to ride. I love horses."

"Me, too," Lauren said. "Moonshine's for sale, you know," she added carefully.

She knew she'd only just met Michael, but she was already beginning to think that he might make a good Unicorn Friend.

"For sale?" Michael echoed. His face lit up briefly, then faded. "Jodie and Chris — Mom and Dad — would never buy her for me."

"Well, ponies are expensive to buy and look after," Lauren agreed.

Michael shook his head. "Oh, it's not the money. It's just that they're not horse people. When I started living with them I asked if I could go to a riding school, but they didn't take me seriously. They said that I would get bored and offered to buy me a bike and a skateboard instead."

Michael looked sadly at Moonshine.

"Jodie and Chris are really nice, but they don't understand me at all. . . ." He broke off, as if he'd said too much. "Look, I'd better go," he muttered. "I'll see you."

"I'm Lauren," Lauren said, realizing she hadn't told him her name.

"See you, Lauren," Michael said, and immediately set off at a run.

"Wait! Where do you live?" Lauren called after him.

But Michael didn't stop. Climbing over the gate, he disappeared into the darkness. Lauren stared after him until she heard a familiar whicker.

Looking around, she saw Twilight walking out from the cover of the trees. It was clear from his expression that he had heard everything.

"Michael doesn't sound very happy," he said, joining Lauren and Moonshine.

Lauren shook here head. "No. It must be difficult having to get used to new parents and not knowing anyone around here."

"Apart from Moonshine," Twilight

said, nuzzling the gray pony, who nuzzled him back before staring wistfully after Michael. She whickered softly.

"Moonshine says she really likes him," Twilight said. "He's kind and gentle."

"And lonely," Lauren said. She sighed and looked at the little gray pony. Both Moonshine and Michael were so unhappy. She wished she and Twilight could help. But what could they do?

CHAPTER

Four

The following morning, Lauren had just finished her breakfast when Mr. Parker arrived. As she got into the back of his car, it was obvious that Jessica and Samantha hadn't come to an agreement on which pony they should have. They were sitting, their arms crossed, arguing with each other.

"We're getting Bullfinch," Samantha was saying.

Jessica frowned. "No, Sandy."

"That's enough, you two," Mr. Parker warned. "The idea of buying a pony was that you would have something to enjoy together, not to spend your time fighting over. If you're going to quarrel, we can just forget this pony idea completely."

Jessica and Samantha quickly stopped arguing.

There was silence for a few minutes and then Jessica looked at her sister. "Please, Samantha," she said quietly. "Please can we get Sandy? You heard what Tina said yesterday — she's only six, so she'll learn to jump better as she gets older. And I really, really like her."

Samantha didn't say anything.

"We could have lessons on her, couldn't we, Dad?" Jessica asked.

Mr. Parker nodded. "Definitely — in fact, I think that would be a very good idea."

"Then I guess she would improve, and she is pretty," Samantha admitted. She frowned. "OK, Jess, I'll think about it."

Jessica exchanged hopeful looks with Lauren, and they traveled the rest of the way in silence.

Lauren stared out the window. She couldn't stop thinking about Michael. She wished she knew where he lived. If she did, she could visit with Twilight. Maybe they could fly back to Moonshine's field that night and see if he visited again.

When they arrived at High Meadows Farm, they saw that Tina

was lunging Sandy in the training ring.
The pony's golden coat gleamed in the
sunlight and her thick, creamy-white tail
floated out behind her. Her neck was
arched and her dainty ears were pricked.

"Look, Sam!" Jessica exclaimed.
"Look how beautiful Sandy looks."

Mr. Parker stopped the car. Samantha,
Jessica, and Lauren jumped out and went
over to the fence.

Seeing them, Tina waved. "Hi there,"
she called, bringing the pony to a halt.
"Do you want to try Sandy and Bullfinch
again?"

Jessica and Lauren looked at Samantha.

"Can we just try Sandy, please?"
Samantha said to Tina.

★ ★ ★

Samantha and Jessica took turns riding Sandy. She was lively but obedient, and she jumped perfectly. By the time they had finished, Samantha was smiling.

"I like her," she said, riding the pony over to the gate and halting her. "She's been much better today."

"And she'll continue to improve," Tina said. "You'll be able to do a lot with her."

Jess turned to her dad. "Can we have her, Dad? Please!"

"If it's all right with Sam, then OK!" Mr. Parker smiled.

"Oh, thank you!" Jessica gasped. She turned to Samantha. "And thank you for agreeing."

"That's OK," Samantha said happily. "I really like her, too, now that I've ridden her again."

While the girls put Sandy back in her stall, Mr. Parker sorted out a price with Tina. It was arranged that she would deliver Sandy the next day.

"I can't believe she's going to be ours," Jessica said as they got into the car.

"She's wonderful," Samantha said, looking genuinely pleased.

Mr. Parker smiled. "Well, I'm glad you two are in agreement at last. Come on, let's go home."

As they turned out of the stables onto the quiet country road, something caught Lauren's eye. A boy with untidy dark hair

was riding a bike up and down the
driveway of a nearby house. It was
Michael! That must be where he was
staying with his family!

She turned in her seat. Michael was
cycling in circles, looking bored.

"What are you looking at?" Jessica asked, following her gaze.

"Nothing," Lauren said quickly.

To her relief, Jessica didn't press any more. She squeezed Lauren's arm. "It's awesome that Samantha and I are going to keep Sandy at Mel's, isn't it? We'll be able to ride together every day."

"Yeah, it'll be great," Lauren agreed. Mel Cassidy was one of their friends. She lived on the farm next door to Lauren, but she was away at summer camp at the moment. Jessica started to talk about everything they would do together when Mel got back. Lauren listened vaguely but her thoughts were on Michael. Now that she knew where

he lived, maybe she could ride over on
Twilight to visit him. It wouldn't be that
far if they went through the woods
instead of going around by the roads.
Michael could have a ride on Twilight.
Determination filled Lauren. She was
going to help him. She was going to be
his friend.

It took Lauren and Twilight just over half
an hour to reach Michael's house through
the woods. A narrow trail brought them
out onto the road beside his house.

As they rode along it, Lauren heard a
woman's voice coming from the yard.
"What would you like to do, Michael?
We could go swimming."

There was no reply.

"Well, how about we go to the park?" Lauren heard the woman say.

"Yeah, I guess," Michael replied quietly. Suddenly, he spoke again. "There's a pony! I can hear a pony coming!"

He came running down the driveway. Recognizing Lauren, his eyes widened.

Lauren waved. "Hi!"

"It's . . . it's you!" Michael stammered in surprise.

Lauren grinned. "Yes, and this is my pony, Twilight. Do you like him?"

Michael nodded, looking astonished. "I didn't know you had a pony."

"You left last night before I could tell you," Lauren explained.

"He looks just like Moonshine," Michael said.

Just then, a slim woman in her thirties with short dark hair came down the driveway. She wore a pretty lilac sundress with matching sandals. This must be Jodie, Michael's adoptive mom. "Who are you talking to, Michael?" She stopped in surprise when she saw Twilight and Lauren.

"My name's Lauren Foster," Lauren said in her politest voice. "I met Michael yesterday —"

"When I went out for a walk," Michael put in quickly.

"I thought I'd come by and say hi," Lauren said. "I hope you don't mind."

"No, no, of course not," Jodie said quickly.

"Michael told me he liked horses and I thought he might like a ride on my pony, Twilight," Lauren said. "We could ride in the woods." She looked at Michael. "If you bring your bike we could take turns riding Twilight."

Michael's face lit up. "Great!" He turned to Jodie. "I can, can't I?"

Jodie looked unsure. "Well, are you sure you want to, honey?"

"Yes!" Michael exclaimed. "Please can I?"

Jodie looked taken aback. "Well, I guess so." She glanced rather dubiously at Twilight. "He is safe, isn't he?"

"Very," Lauren said. "And Michael can wear my helmet."

"Well, OK, then," Jodie said. "But don't be out too long."

"Let's go into the woods," Lauren said

as Michael pushed his bike down the driveway to join her.

"This is fantastic!" Michael said, looking incredibly happy. "How did you know where we were staying?"

Lauren explained about visiting the stables with Jessica's family. "I saw you and thought I'd come visit."

They reached the main trail. Lauren stopped Twilight and dismounted. "Here, you have a turn," she said, handing her riding hat to Michael.

He put it on and mounted. "Wow!" he said, beaming. "It's amazing to be on a pony again."

"You can trot and canter if you want," Lauren said. "Twilight's very good."

To start with, Michael just walked, but as his confidence grew he trotted and cantered. He wasn't a very experienced rider, but his hands were light on the reins and he had very good balance. At last he reined Twilight in. His eyes were shining and his cheeks were flushed. "That was great! Twilight's fantastic, Lauren!"

Lauren smiled. "I know. I'm really lucky."

They rode for a while longer before Michael glanced at his watch. "I guess I should be getting back."

They headed to his house. Jodie was standing on the front porch, looking out for them. "There you are," she said, coming down the steps toward them. "I was starting to worry."

Michael looked at the ground. "Sorry," he mumbled.

"It's OK," Jodie said quickly. "You must be hungry after your ride. Would you like some cookies? I baked them this morning."

"Yes, please," Lauren said.

Michael just nodded.

Lauren looked at him in surprise. He had been chatty out in the woods but now he was quiet. Jodie went inside.

"Your new mom seems really nice," Lauren said in a low voice as she tied Twilight up to the fence at the side of the house.

"She is," Michael said. There was a

flatness in his voice. "Both she and Chris are." He sat down on the porch steps.

Lauren heard a note of reservation in his voice. "But . . . ?" she asked, sitting down beside him.

For a moment, Michael seemed to be wondering whether to say anything more. "But they like different things from me," he said with a sigh. "And that makes it hard."

"What do you mean?" Lauren asked curiously.

"Well, Chris is really into baseball," Michael replied, "and he's always suggesting we go out and practice. And Jodie's always trying to get me to go swimming. I want to please them, so I go along with them, but really I just want to be with horses."

"What do they say when you ask if you can go riding?" Lauren said.

Michael shrugged. "I don't really ask. I did once or twice at the beginning, but not anymore."

"Why not?" Lauren demanded in surprise.

"I want to make them happy," Michael said softly. "I want them to be glad they adopted me. . . ."

He broke off as Jodie came out of the house with a tray of drinks and chocolate chip cookies.

"Here we are," she said cheerfully,

putting the tray down on a table on the
porch. "Have a cookie, Lauren."

"Thank you," Lauren said.

Jodie smiled. "You know, I'm really glad Michael's made a friend," she said, sitting down on the steps, too. "What sort of things do you and your friends do during the summer, Lauren?"

"We go to the creek and we go to one another's houses, but most of all we ride," Lauren said. "Most of my friends have ponies."

Jodie frowned. "Really? Goodness. Things are different in the country. I grew up in the city. None of my friends ever rode."

"Maybe Michael could start to ride while you're here," Lauren suggested hopefully.

"Oh, I'm not sure," Jodie said

doubtfully. "You'd probably find it a little boring, wouldn't you, Michael?"

"No!" Michael said, looking up quickly. "I'd love to go riding."

Lauren's eyes suddenly widened. She'd just had a brilliant idea!

CHAPTER

Five

"There are stables just around the corner from here," Lauren burst out, looking at Jodie. "Maybe Michael could help out there for the summer. He'd get to know people and he could be with horses."

"That would be amazing!" Michael gasped. "Can I?" he begged Jodie. "Can I, please?"

Jodie raised her eyebrows. "You wouldn't really want to, would you?"

"Yes," Michael said. "I'd love to."

"Well, I suppose I *could* speak to the owner," Jodie said.

Michael jumped up. "Now?" he asked eagerly.

Jodie looked at him in amazement. "You *are* excited. Well, OK. If it means that much to you then we can go and ask right away." She finished her drink. "I'll just lock the house and get my bag."

Tina was leading Puzzle in from the field when Lauren arrived with Michael and Jodie. Jodie explained what they had come for.

"Michael likes the idea of helping out," she said to Tina. "Do you let children do that?"

"Yes," Tina replied. "I usually have at least five or six of them helping me in exchange for rides. At the moment, several are away at camp. I could use another pair of hands." She looked at Michael. "The trouble is, you're younger than most of my helpers and I won't be able to offer you many rides. I think a lot of the ponies will be too strong for you."

"That's OK," Michael said quickly. "I'd be happy just to help."

Twilight suddenly lifted his head and neighed. From the field by the parking lot came an answering whinny. Tina looked around. Moonshine was standing at the gate, staring at them.

She scratched her head. "I suppose there's always Moonshine," she said. "She's very quiet. You could ride her, Michael."

"I'd love to!" Michael said. He looked at Lauren, his eyes shining.

"OK, then," Tina said. "It's settled. You come and help me with the yard chores and you can ride Moonshine in exchange."

"And can I groom her and clean her tack?" Michael asked eagerly.

Tina smiled at his enthusiasm. "As much as you like."

Lauren was desperate to talk to Twilight about the good news. She couldn't wait until that evening and so on the way

home, she turned him down an
overgrown path that led to a hidden
glade in the woods.

Twilight walked forward eagerly,
pushing his way through the overhanging
branches. At last, the path opened out
into the sunny clearing. The grass was
springy and scattered with purple flowers.
Golden butterflies fluttered through the
warm, sweet-scented air. It was the most
secret place Lauren knew.

She said the Turning Spell.

"So, what do you think?" she asked
as soon as the purple flash faded and
Twilight was standing in front of her in
his unicorn form.

"It's a wonderful idea," Twilight said.

"Moonshine will love having someone to look after her each day."

"And Michael will love helping with all the ponies," Lauren said.

Twilight nodded. "He would make a very good Unicorn Friend."

"I know," Lauren agreed. "But I guess Moonshine's just going to have to wait for someone else to come along. Michael's only here for another five weeks, so he probably won't have time to find out that she's a unicorn."

"Unless we help him," Twilight said thoughtfully.

Lauren frowned. "But we can't, Twilight. You know Unicorn Friends have to find out the truth about their

unicorn by themselves. That's why Mrs.
Fontana could only hint that you were a
unicorn when I got you. We can't tell
Michael. If he's going to be a Unicorn
Friend, he has to believe in magic
enough to try the spell without knowing
whether it will work."

Twilight nodded. "I know, and I didn't
mean that we should tell him everything,
but couldn't we sort of *help* him find out
the truth?"

"I guess so," Lauren said slowly. A
thought struck her. "But if he does find
out, what will happen when he has to
leave Moonshine at the end of the
summer? It will be awful for him."

"But isn't it better he has five weeks as

a Unicorn Friend than none?" Twilight pointed out.

Lauren hesitated. She wasn't sure. It was going to be hard enough for Michael to leave Moonshine at the end of the summer. Surely it would be a hundred times worse if he had to leave her knowing she was a unicorn?

"I don't know," she said uncertainly. She twisted her fingers in Twilight's mane and wondered how she would feel if she had to leave Twilight. *I couldn't bear it,* she thought.

But what if she had never known about his unicorn powers? Not known what it was like to fly through the starry skies, to feel the wind against her face and Twilight's warm back beneath her?

Not even having the memories . . . No, that would be even worse.

Twilight nuzzled her. "What does your heart say, Lauren?"

Lauren hesitated. Yes, it would be dreadful for Michael to have to leave Moonshine at the end of the summer but, like Twilight had said, surely it was better that he did that instead of never knowing the truth. "My heart says that we should help him," she said slowly.

"Well, I think that, too," Twilight said. "So let's do it!"

Lauren looked at him. His dark eyes were eager. She paused and then made a decision.

"OK," she agreed.

As she spoke, she felt a weight drop off her shoulders. She was sure that they were doing the right thing. They should help Michael. The only question was: *How were they going to do it?*

Even though Lauren thought about it all night, by the time she rode Twilight to Tina's the next morning she hadn't come up with an answer. Michael was riding Moonshine in the ring when she arrived. Moonshine was cantering eagerly, her ears pricked.

Michael saw them. "Hi there," he called.

"Moonshine's looking good," Lauren said.

Michael bent down and hugged Moonshine's neck. "She's wonderful."

Tina came across the yard. Seeing Lauren, she smiled. "Hello. Come to visit?"

Lauren nodded. "You don't mind, do you?"

"Not at all," Tina said. She looked at Michael. "That's probably enough ring-work for Moonshine today. Why don't you go out into the woods for a short ride?"

"OK," Michael said eagerly.

He rode out of the yard with Lauren. "So, are you enjoying helping Tina?" she asked.

"It's great," Michael said, his face glowing. "I've mucked out five stables

already this morning. This is going to be the best vacation ever."

Lauren stroked Twilight. Michael's vacation would be even better if he knew about Moonshine. But how could she help him? She couldn't just start talking about unicorns out of the blue — he'd think she was crazy.

Beside her, Michael patted Moonshine's neck. "You know, I'm sure Moonshine understands me when I talk to her," he said. "It's the way she looks at me. Like she's smarter than other ponies." He laughed, sounding suddenly embarrassed. "I guess that sounds really dumb."

"No, it doesn't," Lauren said. "I know

what you mean. Twilight's the same. It's like they're different from other ponies."

She glanced quickly at Michael. Maybe this was her chance to say something more. But what could she say? Before she could think of anything, Michael had pushed Moonshine on.

"Come on, let's canter!" he called.

Twilight jumped forward eagerly.

Lauren had no choice but to let him race after the little gray mare. She felt a wave of frustration at the wasted chance. Michael would be a perfect Unicorn Friend if only he would try the spell. But how could she get him to do that? Maybe if she had lots of time she could think of

a way, but in just five weeks Michael
would be going back to the city.

I'll come up with something, Lauren
thought, crouching low against Twilight's
neck as he cantered along the path. *I just
have to.*

CHAPTER

Six

A week passed by but Lauren didn't get any further in helping Michael work out Moonshine's secret. It was so frustrating. The more she saw him with Moonshine and realized how much he loved the pony, the more she wanted him to be Moonshine's Unicorn Friend. But she just couldn't think of how to help him find out the truth. It seemed impossible.

On Saturday, Michael came to her house and they went down to the creek with Jessica and Samantha. They took turns riding Twilight and Sandy. When they got back to her house they brushed Twilight down and then went up to Lauren's bedroom.

"I like your room," Michael said, looking admiringly at the horse posters Lauren had stuck on the walls. He went over to the window. "Hey, you can see Twilight's paddock from here." Lauren's unicorn book was lying open on the window seat. Michael picked it up and started to leaf through the pages. "Wow! This book looks interesting."

Lauren's heart leaped. Of course! The

book had all the information Michael
needed.

Michael turned the first page. "Look

at this pony! It looks just like Twilight and Moonshine."

"It's a picture of what unicorns look like when they're disguised," Lauren said.

"What do you mean?" Michael asked, looking around at her.

And suddenly, Lauren knew as clearly as anything what she had to do. "Read the book and it'll tell you," she told him. "You can borrow it for the summer."

Michael looked surprised. "Are you sure?"

Lauren nodded. She loved the book and didn't want to let it go — even for a few weeks — but she was sure that it was the only way that Michael was going to learn about unicorns.

"OK, thanks," he said, looking really happy.

"Lauren!" Mrs. Foster called up the stairs. "Michael's mom is here."

"We'd better go," Lauren said. They went downstairs. Jodie was in the kitchen.

"Hi, honey," she said as Michael came in. "Have you had a good day?"

Michael's eyes shone. "It's been great! We rode to the creek with Lauren's friends Jessica and Samantha, and we had a picnic and we swam."

"That sounds fun," Jodie said.

"It was fantastic!" Michael said. He looked around. "I left my bag in your tack room, Lauren. Can I go get it?"

"Sure," Lauren said.

Michael put the unicorn book down on the table and ran outside. Jodie shook her head. "I just can't believe the change in him since we moved out to the country for the summer," she said to Mrs. Foster. "He used to be so quiet, but now he talks all the time — although only about horses."

Mrs. Foster laughed. "That sounds very familiar. Is he going to continue riding when you return to the city?"

"We'll see," Jodie replied. "Kids in the city don't really ride."

Lauren looked at her mom. "I used to ride a lot when we lived in the city, didn't I, Mom?"

Mrs. Foster nodded. "We only moved

here at Easter," she explained to Jodie. "Before then, Lauren used to ride every weekend. I know it's not so easy, but there are riding schools and kids who ride. It's a good hobby — the children learn responsibility and have fun at the same time."

Jodie looked surprised. "Oh, I see."

Michael came back in. "I've got it," he said, waving his bag. He started to put the book carefully inside. "Thanks for having me here, Mrs. Foster."

"It's my pleasure," Mrs. Foster replied.

"What have you got there?" Jodie asked Michael, looking at the book.

"Lauren lent it to me," Michael answered. "It's a book about unicorns."

Lauren sensed her mom glance quickly at her. Her mom knew that the unicorn book was one of the most precious things Lauren owned.

"Well, thank you very much, Lauren," Jodie said.

"I'm sure Michael will take very good care of it."

Lauren nodded and she and her mom saw Jodie and Michael to their car.

"So?" her mom said quietly to her as they waved them off.

"So?" Lauren said, but she knew what her mom was getting at.

"The book," Mrs. Foster said, looking at her. "You love that book, Lauren. I'm surprised you're letting it out of your sight."

"I know," Lauren said. "But Michael was looking at it today and he really liked it and . . ." She hesitated. "And I wanted to lend it to him for the summer."

Her mom looked at her for a moment.

Then she smiled. "There's a lot of good in you, Lauren Foster," she said, hugging her. "I'm proud you're my daughter." She kissed Lauren's hair.

"Mom!" Lauren protested, but she felt a warm glow inside.

They walked back into the house.

"Michael really does love ponies, doesn't he?" Mrs. Foster said. "I guess it must be strange for his parents if they've never been into horses themselves and don't know anyone who rides. It probably seems an odd thing for him to want to do. Still, maybe if they see how much he enjoys himself this summer they'll let him continue riding when they go home."

Lauren nodded. But she couldn't really think about Michael going back to the city. Right now all that mattered was his finding out Moonshine's secret. Would he read the book? And, even more important, would he believe it? Lauren crossed her fingers. She and Twilight were just going to have to wait and see.

As Lauren rode Twilight over to High Meadows Farm early the next morning, she said, "I wonder if Michael read the book last night." A thought struck her. "What if he doesn't believe it? I had the book for ages before I tried turning you into a unicorn, Twilight." She thought back to that time. "It was only when I

saw the moonflowers in the secret glade
that I started to wonder if the spell might
actually work," she said.

Twilight stopped dead.

"What's wrong?" Lauren said.

To her surprise, Twilight turned
around and started heading back down
the track. "What are you doing?" Lauren
asked in astonishment.

Twilight broke into a trot. Lauren
quickly loosened the reins. It was clear
he'd had an idea about something,
although she didn't know what. She let
him go where he wanted.

He trotted down the path for about two
minutes, finally halting by the overgrown
trail that led to the secret glade.

"Why have you stopped here?" Lauren said.

Twilight started to walk down the trail. Lauren ducked under the branches, wondering what he was doing. As soon as they entered the glade, he plunged his head down to the ground.

"You came here because you wanted to eat some grass?" Lauren said in surprise. Twilight stamped his hoof and she suddenly realized that he wasn't eating. He was nudging a moonflower with his nose.

Her eyes widened as she finally understood. "You think we should take a moonflower to Michael?"

Twilight nodded.

"It's a brilliant idea!" Lauren said. "He probably just thinks they're made-up flowers in the book, but if I give one to him he'll see that they really exist and maybe it'll make him try the spell." She jumped off and picked a flower.

Twilight tossed his head as if to say, *That's what I thought all along.* Putting the flower in her pocket, Lauren remounted and they continued on their way.

Moonshine was tied up in the yard at High Meadows Farm. Lauren noticed how much better she was looking. Her coat was now sleek and gray and her mane and tail were silky.

Michael came out of a barn with a

wheelbarrow. He was
deep in thought.

"Hi," Lauren called.

Michael looked up. "Oh . . . hi."

"Are you free to go for a ride?" Lauren
asked.

"I've got another two stalls to muck out first," Michael said. "But then I can."

Lauren dismounted. "I'll give you a hand." She tied Twilight up by Moonshine and then set to work, watching Michael carefully all the time.

For a while, Michael worked in silence, but at last he spoke. "I was reading that book last night."

Lauren glanced at him eagerly. "What did you think?"

"It was really good." He laughed in an embarrassed way. "I mean, I know it's not true or anything, but it's a really good story."

Lauren remembered the flower. It was now or never. "I brought you something

from the woods." She took the
moonflower out of her jeans. The gold
spots on the tip of each purple petal
seemed to glow in the light of the stall.

Michael looked as if he was wondering
why she had brought him a flower, but
then his eyes widened. "It's a . . . it's a . . ."

"Moonflower," Lauren murmured.

Michael's eyes flew to hers. "They really exist?"

Lauren nodded. "Yes, and so does the Twilight Star. It shines every night for ten minutes just after the sun sets." She met his eyes. "You just have to believe."

Michael stared.

Fearing that in a minute she'd tell him everything, Lauren pushed the flower into his hand. "Here, take it. I'll empty the wheelbarrow." Before he could ask her any questions, she grabbed the handles of the wheelbarrow and pushed it out of the stall.

Michael didn't say much for the rest of the morning. He seemed to be thinking hard, and even when they went out on a ride, he remained quiet. On the way home, Lauren caught him looking from Moonshine to Twilight. *Oh, please,* she thought, *try the spell tonight.*

They got back to the yard to find Jodie coming out of the office with Tina.

Seeing the surprise on Michael's face, Jodie smiled. "Don't worry, nothing's wrong. I just thought I'd come see Tina and find out how you were doing."

"And I said you were doing great," Tina said. "Moonshine's been like a different pony since you started looking after her, Michael."

"So, this is Moonshine?" Jodie asked, looking interested.

"Yes," Michael answered. "Isn't she perfect?"

Jodie stroked Moonshine. "Oh, she is pretty."

"She's the best," Michael said, leaning forward and hugging the little gray pony. "Aren't you, girl? She understands everything."

Lauren patted Twilight's neck. If only Michael knew how true that was . . .

CHAPTER

Seven

The next morning, Lauren was up and out of the house by nine o'clock. She was longing to see Michael.

Michael was grooming Moonshine when Lauren rode into the yard at High Meadows Farm. The little pony's coat looked even glossier and her dark eyes had a new sparkle.

"Hi," Lauren called eagerly.

Michael swung around. "Hello!" The word almost burst out of him. He looked very excited. "Lauren!" he said, running over. "I've got to tell you something! Something amazing about Moonshine. She's a —"

"Shh," Lauren interrupted, quickly dismounting. "I know."

Michael stared at her. "What do you mean, you know?"

Lauren looked pointedly at Twilight. He followed her gaze and his eyes widened. "Twilight's a —"

"You can't tell anyone," Lauren broke in. "No one can know about him or Moonshine. You can't talk about it — not to anyone. It's got to be a secret."

"But . . . but . . ." Michael stammered.

"Remember what the book said," Lauren reminded him.

They stared at each other for a moment.

"I can't believe it's true," Michael said, shaking his head in wonder.

Lauren smiled. "It is. Believe me, it is."

Just then, Tina came out of the barn. She was showing a man and a dark-haired girl around the yard.

Lauren stiffened. "I know that girl. She's named Monica Corder. She's in my class at school. What's she doing here?"

Michael looked surprised. "She and
her dad are looking for a pony, I think."

"She's not very nice," Lauren said.

"There's nothing here," Monica was
saying loudly to her dad. "I want a pony
that's going to win things."

"Well, how about that chestnut with
the blaze?" Mr. Corder said. He turned to
Tina. "You said he'd won a lot lately."

Monica folded her arms. "But I don't want a chestnut, I want a gray."

"Why don't you just give him a try, Monica?" Mr. Corder said.

"I guess I could," Monica said grudgingly.

"Michael," Tina called. "Can you tack up Puzzle for me, please?"

Monica glanced in their direction. Seeing Lauren, she frowned in surprise. "Lauren! What are you doing here?" she said, speaking as if Lauren had no right to be in Tina's yard. Before Lauren could reply, Monica's eyes had fallen on Moonshine. "Hey! What's *that* pony's name?" she demanded.

"Moonshine," Michael replied.

Monica's gaze swept over Moonshine's soft gray coat and silky mane and tail. "I like her," she declared. She turned to her father. "Dad! I like this pony. She's really pretty. I'll try her, too."

Lauren and Michael stared at each other in horror.

Mr. Corder turned to Tina. "We'll have that one saddled up, too, please."

"Well, actually," Tina said, stepping forward, "I've already got someone booked to see that pony later this morning. They've asked to be given first refusal on her — that means they have first choice on whether to buy her or not," she explained to Monica. "So although you can try her out, I have to wait and let the other people see her as well."

Lauren stared at Tina. There were other people who wanted Moonshine? But they couldn't. Moonshine couldn't be sold! Especially not now that Michael had discovered her secret.

Monica scowled. "But I like her best."

"I'm sorry, but that's the situation," Tina said.

"Well, I'll try her, anyway," Monica said.

Tina turned to Michael. "Can you tack up Moonshine as well, please, Michael?"

Michael looked totally shocked as he got the tack. Lauren felt awful. Poor

Michael. What would he do if
Moonshine was sold?

Monica mounted Moonshine. She landed
with a thump in the saddle and
Moonshine took a surprised step
backward.

"Walk on!" Monica said sharply,
digging her heels into Moonshine's sides.

When Moonshine didn't respond immediately, Monica smacked her with her riding crop. Moonshine jumped forward in alarm. Lauren glanced at Michael. His face was pale.

"Just give her time to get used to you, Monica," Tina called, standing by the gate with Puzzle.

Monica dug her heels in again. "Come on."

Moonshine's walk slowed down. Monica smacked her again with her crop. "Walk on!"

But Moonshine just got slower and slower. Although she was very good for Michael, she seemed determined to be as lazy as possible for Monica.

After a circuit of the ring, Monica stopped Moonshine by the gate. "She's a useless pony," she said scathingly. "She's so slow." She dismounted. "She's way too lazy for me."

Lauren felt a rush of relief.

"Oh, well, never mind," Tina said cheerfully. "I think the people who are coming later this morning will be just perfect for her."

Lauren glanced at her. Tina didn't sound like she cared about Michael's feelings. Surely she knew how upset he was at the thought of Moonshine being sold?

"I'll try the other pony instead," Monica said.

As she mounted Puzzle, Tina turned to
Michael. "Seeing as Moonshine's tacked
up, why don't you take her out for a quick
ride in the woods, Michael? The other
people won't be here for a while, and you
can clean her up when you get back."

Michael nodded. Lauren realized that
Tina had suggested the ride to be kind
because she could see that Michael was
only just managing to fight back his tears.

As they rode out of the yard, Lauren
looked at him. "I'm really sorry," she said.

Michael stared at Moonshine's mane.
"She can't be sold," he said in a low,
trembling voice.

"At least Monica didn't want her,"
Lauren said, trying to cheer him up.

"And maybe she'll be just as lazy for these other people, then they won't want her, either." She leaned forward. "Moonshine. You've got to do exactly what you did with Monica this afternoon. These people *can't* buy you."

Moonshine nodded slightly.

"And maybe we can put these people off her," Lauren said, trying to think of something. "Tell them that she's naughty or something."

"Yes." Michael looked suddenly hopeful, but then his face fell. "I won't be here. Jodie and Chris are taking me shopping later."

"Well, I'll stay," Lauren said. "I'll try and think of something."

Michael swallowed. "I know I've got to say good-bye to Moonshine at the end of the summer, but not now, especially not after finding out that she's a —"

"Shh!" Lauren said quickly in case there was anyone nearby in the woods who might overhear.

She saw a tear fall down Michael's face. "I'll think of something," she said desperately. "I promise."

CHAPTER

Eight

As Lauren and Michael rode back to the yard, Tina came out of a barn. "Great, you're back. Can you brush Moonshine and oil her hooves, Michael?"

"Did Monica buy Puzzle?" Lauren asked.

Tina shook her head. "She didn't like him, although at least he was better behaved than Moonshine." She walked over and patted the little gray pony next to Michael. "I've never known you to be so lazy, girl. I guess you just didn't like her."

Leaving Michael to clean up Moonshine, Tina went to the tack room. Lauren tried desperately to think of a plan.

"I'm going to have to go in a minute," Michael said, looking at his watch after he'd oiled Moonshine's hooves. "Have you thought of anything, Lauren?"

She shook her head. "Not yet."

"What am I going to do?" he said.

Just then, there was the sound of a car coming down the driveway. Tina came out of the tack room. "Ah, here are the people to see Moonshine."

Michael and Lauren turned around to look at the black car.

"No it's not, Tina. It's my mom and dad," Michael said. "They must have decided to come and get me. We're going shopping."

"Yes," Tina said with a smile. "I know."

Lauren looked at her. There was something about the way she was smiling. . . .

Michael had obviously noticed it, too. He looked from Tina to his mom and dad, who were parking the car. "What . . . what's going on?" he asked.

"Yes, you're going shopping, Michael — for a pony," Tina told him.

Both Lauren and Michael stared at her.

"A pony!" Michael gasped.

Tina nodded. "When your mom came to see me yesterday, it was to talk about buying you Moonshine. I suggested she come with your dad to see her today."

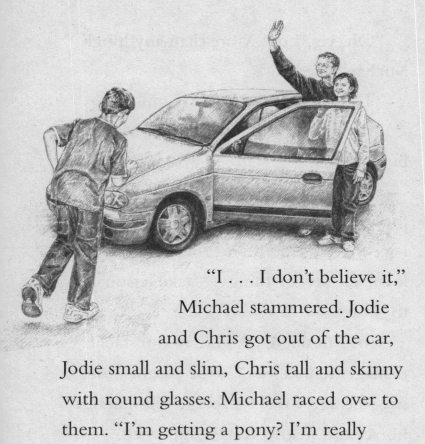

"I . . . I don't believe it,"
Michael stammered. Jodie
and Chris got out of the car,
Jodie small and slim, Chris tall and skinny
with round glasses. Michael raced over to
them. "I'm getting a pony? I'm really
getting Moonshine?" His eyes looked
almost wild.

"If you want her," Jodie said.

"Oh, yes, I do! More than anything!" Michael cried.

"Then she's yours." Chris smiled.

"But where will I keep her?" Michael burst out.

"I phoned some stables in the city and found one near home," Jodie said. "They have a pony club there. You'll be able to learn all sorts of things — take lessons, go to shows."

Chris nodded. "And they run stable management classes for the parents, too, so Jodie and I will be able to learn about horses and help you." He squeezed Michael's shoulder. "If you want us to, of course."

Michael looked almost lost for words.

"That . . . that would be great." He swung around. "Lauren! Did you hear that?"

She grinned at him. "Yes. It's great!"

Michael grabbed hold of Jodie's and Chris's hands. "Come see Moonshine," he said, half pulling them across the yard.

Moonshine whickered as they got close. Michael ran over and patted her proudly. "You're going to be mine!" he told her.

"We just want you to be happy," Jodie said to him, smiling at his joyful face. "It's all we've ever wanted. We only tried to get you to do things like baseball and swimming because we thought you'd enjoy them."

"I know," Michael said. "It's just that I like horses."

"I guess we only realized that once we saw how much you've liked coming and helping here," Chris said. "I mean, before that you'd only mentioned riding once or twice."

"I know." Michael looked awkward. "It was because you didn't seem to like the idea when I did mention it, so I stopped. I wanted to please you and do what you wanted."

"I think we've all been trying a bit too hard," Jodie said. "Maybe now the three of us can really start being a family." She walked forward and patted the little gray pony. "Sorry, I should have said the four of us, of course. Welcome to the family, Moonshine."

Moonshine whickered softly and Michael threw his arms around Jodie and Chris in delight. They hugged him tightly.

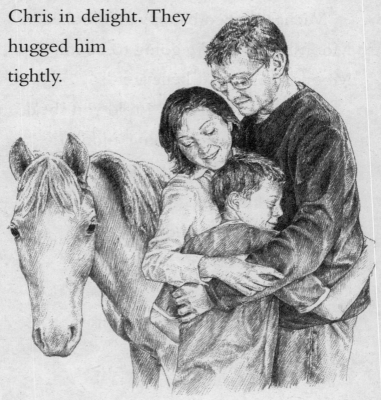

Lauren's thoughts were whirling. She could hardly believe that after she and Michael had been so worried, things had all ended perfectly.

Michael sighed happily and looked at Moonshine. "You're going to be mine, Moonshine! I can't believe it!"

Tina smiled at him. "I told you she'd be going to a perfect home, didn't I?"

Michael nodded. "But I didn't know you meant me. I'm so lucky. She's the best pony in the world!"

Twilight snorted.

"One of the two best ponies in the world," Michael corrected himself.

The adults laughed.

"Everyone thinks their pony is the best pony in the world," Tina commented.

Michael grinned at Lauren. "But in our case it's true, isn't it?"

Lauren grinned back. "Definitely," she said.

The night air was warm and still as Lauren and Twilight stood in the shadow of the trees, waiting for Michael to visit Moonshine. Twilight bent to rub his head against his knee as a shaft of moonlight shone down through the branches and glanced off his pearly horn.

"He's coming," Lauren whispered. "Look."

Twilight lifted his head. Michael was
hurrying down the driveway.

Moonshine was waiting by the gate.
She whinnied softly, her ears pricked.

Michael climbed the gate and stood

beside her, his hand on her gray neck.
Lauren saw his lips move. Suddenly, there
was a bright purple flash and Moonshine
was transformed into a unicorn. She was
beautiful; her long tail swept almost to

the ground and her coat gleamed like
mother-of-pearl in the moonlight.

"What should we do?" Twilight
murmured. "Do you think we should go
over and say hello?"

Lauren looked at Michael and
Moonshine. They were standing only
inches apart, their heads almost touching.
They looked lost in their own little
world.

"No," Lauren said suddenly. "Let's
leave them."

As she spoke, Michael got onto
Moonshine's back. Moonshine turned
and, pushing off with her hind legs, she
cantered up into the sky. Lauren smiled,
her eyes shining. At long last, Moonshine

had found a true Unicorn Friend, and it
wasn't just for the summer. It looked like
they were going to be together for a long,

long time to come — just like Twilight and her.

As she turned Twilight toward home, Lauren buried her face in his silvery mane. They had so many more wonderful adventures ahead of them — she couldn't wait!

Make sure to look for more adventures with Lauren and Twilight in . . .

A Winter Wish

Max was busy playing with Walter, and Lauren waited to see if Mrs. Fontana would come and find her. Sure enough, a few minutes later, the store owner came into the children's section. "How's Twilight?" she asked.

"He's fine," Lauren replied.

Their eyes met and Mrs. Fontana

dropped her voice. "Have you been out flying much?"

"Every night," Lauren whispered.

Mrs. Fontana smiled. "It should snow soon and then you'll really have fun. I remember the first time I flew in snow. It was wonderful." For a moment she looked lost in memories. She shook her head and focused on Lauren again. "Enjoy it," she said softly. "I promise you it'll be an experience you won't forget."

"Lauren!"

Hearing her mom, Lauren quickly turned around. "Yes?" she said, trying to look as normal as possible.

Mrs. Foster came into the children's

section. "Why don't you choose a couple of books for Carla and Anna?"

"OK, thanks. That's a good idea!" Lauren replied.

"Carla and Anna?" Mrs. Fontana echoed as Mrs. Foster left to go back to the adults section, and Lauren started looking at the shelf of pony books.

"They were my best friends when I lived in the city," Lauren explained. "They're coming to stay on Saturday, and we're going to do lots of Christmassy things." She felt a rush of excitement. "I can't wait to see them! We've been friends since we were four."

"That's good." Mrs. Fontana said. "Friends are very important." Her bright eyes studied Lauren for a moment. "All friends — old ones and new ones, special ones, and even four-legged ones. They all have a part to play in our lives."

Lauren wasn't sure what she meant. "Yes," she agreed hesitantly.

Mrs. Fontana smiled. "Well, I'm sure you'll have a wonderful time." She spoke more briskly. "Now what kinds of books do they like?"

With Mrs. Fontana's help, Lauren chose pony stories for Carla and Anna. Mrs. Foster paid and then she, Lauren, and Max went back out to the car.

As they drove home, her mom put a tape of Christmas songs on. Gazing at the decorated store fronts flashing by in a